This is a story of a true event which happened in a little village in Sussex whilst driving home from work (I looked after an elderly lady).

After shutting her kitchen door, the security light came on, which was an asset when it was dark. But this particular evening it wasn't dark at all, and as I sat in my car outside I looked right and saw what appeared to be a balloon: a very large balloon with a smaller balloon on top. I sat there wondering and saw them seem to attempt to push open a gate leading into a field and then carry on bumbling along down a lane towards me...

JULES STEVENS

Bubble and Squeak

AUSTIN MACAULEY PUBLISHERS™
LONDON • CAMBRIDGE • NEW YORK • SHARJAH

A CIP catalogue record for this title is available from the British Library.

ISBN 9781035823710 (Paperback)
ISBN 9781035823727 (ePub-e-book)

www.austinmacauley.com

First Published 2023
Austin Macauley Publishers Ltd
1 Canada Square
Canary Wharf
London
E14 5AA

I T WAS DARK, and I had finished working for an elderly lady in the countryside, in the middle of nowhere. I had helped her to bed, got her a drink, sorted out her oxygen, and now it was time to leave. I never liked leaving because she lived in the country, surrounded by fields and gates and lanes. So, I made my way downstairs to the kitchen door and got out my torch in order to get to my car before the security light came on, and then it was a deep breath and off. I went up and down the garden rockery, missing the pathway and heading for the car, which now shone like a car in a salesroom.

This night, it wasn't too dark for some reason, and I was able to see quite clearly the road ahead both ways. My employer lived in a triangle, so I could travel either way, but as I looked right, I was made aware of two large balloons just bumbling along together, and I began to laugh, thinking someone had had a party and let them go, but then I noticed them both stop at a gate and bounce back and forth, obviously trying to push it open. Then they gave up and so started bumbling down the road again towards me and the lane leading down to the crossroads. I began to wonder what this was, so I started the car and drove down the lane ahead. This turned off into another lane, which headed towards a crossroads. I wondered whether our paths might cross, and indeed, as I slowly made my way along the road, I could smell this atrocious stench emanating from the lane, and there before my eyes bumbling along was a creature with another creature on top, two massive balloon-type creatures bouncing along the road and heading for the lane in front that had a gate open. The creature was orange and translucent, but I could see floating stuff inside and, notably, a square blue pocket in the corner. As they both saw me, they, detecting the small object on top, acknowledged my presence as I waited for them to cross the road. The smell was indeed overwhelming, and as I waited for them to cross I put the car into gear, and then sped off.

I was in my 60s and newly diagnosed with Parkinson's Disease. I had experienced hallucinations but only at night, around 4.00 a.m., which my Parkinson's Nurse knew all about. How could I express my 'encounter' without anyone judging me as deluded due to my condition? Furthermore, any such sighting would never be understood, and people who generally talk about such a happening are never taken seriously. So I decided that I wouldn't say anything to anyone and just get on with life as a Care Assistant in a hospital studying for a degree in Humanistic Counselling at university, together with visiting my sick mother in a care home.

The years went past quite quickly. My mother had died, and I had finished my studies at university and decided to take early retirement. One day, after reading to my grandchildren, I decided to write a children's book based on my encounter with the bubbles whilst working for an elderly lady. I put together a children's book called *Bubble and Squeak*. I based it on my experience but obviously added to it wildly with information I had later found out about in that area. I made out that the story was indeed a fairy tale and had a happy ending, which was further from the truth than anything. I went on to adapt: "Bubble and Squeak were never apart, always together in a farmer's field, but only at night because at night they didn't get pestered by humans and were able to roam freely. They had a mission every day to pick up stones from the area, little crumb-like stones to take back to base. 'Base' was an old farm that had an opening in a rock which allowed Bubble and Squeak through. Once they had gone through this aperture, no one knew what happened to them until the following night at 6.00 p.m. At 6.00 p.m., they would come out of the rocks and bumble up the road bouncing off one another and heading for their usual place, waiting at the crossroads to cross the road. Once over the crossing, they would go up the road into a field and see their families."

However, this idyllic parody did not take place at all. I never realised that my picture was taken along with other dimensions that night, now six years ago, and the stench that they, the aliens, were covered in was, in fact, fuel, ready to explode on impact if anything got in their way. The stories that I made up were, in fact, partially true. The bubbles were looking for minerals, diamonds to be exact, and scoured the earth, particularly farms that had outhouses not used so they could bury themselves underground sufficiently that no one could see them. It was also true that farmers were too scared to notify anyone because of their demeanour and presence. It seemed that they killed anything that got in their way, as one could see the aftermath of such atrocities, such as burned-out cars and skeletons of animal and human forms which littered the way up to the farmhouse. This was a true story.

Of course, the authorities got involved, especially looking inside the farmhouse and closing it off but leaving unanswered questions everywhere and sealing off the farm completely, even though there were many rabbits and foxes lying by the side of the road, intoxicated by fumes. Then it happened for real: a farmer, walking his sheepdog through his fields, was found lying down in his field with the sheep and dog dead around him. Again, the district council and county council tried to find out what had caused his demise, but nothing surfaced, so nothing happened, and there were no real answers. People around that area didn't pursue it, so it was laid bare for imaginations to run wild, as mine did.

The farmhouse was still a mystery and guarded by 'Trespassing' and 'No Entry' signs. It was still in my mind until, one day, I walked along the promenade on my own, a place that I used to run up and down without getting exhausted, but now the deterioration of Parkinson's had taken over, and a walk was quite sufficient for my aching legs and muscles. As I was clearly the only one on the prom that Sunday morning and looking out onto an abysmal foggy sea, suddenly I began to smell that smell again, the one that I encountered at the site of the old girl I looked after. The smell was there and getting stronger. I looked around and couldn't see anything, until out of the clouds an orange bubble appeared and bounced itself towards me. I stepped back, and it stopped. This was just one bubble, not carrying the other small one on its shoulders. It began to circle me, and I stepped back again, and so it stopped. Out of the blue pouch it carried on itself were stones, small grey stones. It left around five of them.

I looked at them and said out loud, "What are these?"

A muffled voice said, "Diamonds."

I said, "Are these for me?"

"Yes," it said, "we want more, we use them, show us where to get some."

I said, "There are no diamond mines here in the UK. The only diamonds are in the shops, jewellery shops."

It said, "Show me," so I got out my mobile phone and showed it Tiffany's, for a start, and as I went through my phone, it bounced back into the sky. I began to tremble all over and looked around for onlookers, but there was no one. I walked back to my flat and had a shower, as I could still feel or smell the odour of that mysterious alien.

The next day was a Monday, and around 7 a.m. I turned on the news and found that the entire Tiffany shops around the world had been targeted and robbed of all their jewellery. No injuries took place, but it had me thinking that now I was somehow an accomplice to my bouncy aliens, and I knew that a walk on the promenade was definitely not on my keeping fit regime. The next day I walked on the promenade again to see if the bubble was around, as I was now intrigued by its presence and need for diamonds. Within minutes it appeared on the other side of the railings on the promenade.

"Show me how to cycle; I want to learn," it bellowed out to me. I covered my face with astonishment, and Bubble said, "No one else can see me but you, so don't worry."

"Oh, that's okay then, I did wonder. And besides, if you want to cycle, you will need two arms and two legs, just like me."

The Bubble bounced back into the clouds and showed itself again and said, "We don't have any."

"No, I don't suppose you would; well, thank goodness you don't." There was silence, and I said, "Hey, there are manikins in the skips of some shops. We could go see if any may help you".

"I will follow you, I am always with you."

I said okay and walked back to my flat to get the car. Once travelling with Bubble out of view, I saw a skip at the back of Asda and noticed two male manikins. I quickly took the arms and the legs and put them in the back of my car. Suddenly Bubble swooped down, snatched them out of my boot and disappeared. I headed off back to my flat, parked the car and walked back down to the promenade. By this point, I had no idea that onlookers were looking at someone and talking to themselves, but I figured as long as I had a mobile and earpiece, this could have been a natural procedure. Then out of the blue, Bubble appeared with legs and arms, and to my amazement, it had hands that actually worked.

"Well done," I said, "this is great." So now Bubble walked next to me in a way appropriate to someone with bandy legs and almost took over the pavement. I had very little room.

"We need the bicycles. Where are they"?

I told him that bicycles were very expensive and we would have to return to the skips somewhere to find them.

"I will give you this," Bubble produced the biggest emerald I had ever seen.

"OMG," I said, "this is worth hundreds and thousands. You want me to use this?"

"Yes, whatever it takes," said Bubble.

I told him the shops were shut now and that I needed to eat but would meet him again tomorrow at the same time and place. I returned home as Bubble bounced its way into the clouds, and me holding this whopping emerald stone. The next day I went to a nearby jeweller and showed them this raw uncut emerald. They were aghast at its size and translucent appearance. I had already made up a story about heirloom stuff, and the assistant took it backstage, as it were, to get me a price. She came back and told me the item was indeed quite priceless and said for me to go to London, in Soho, to get a price and insure it straight away. I asked for an estimated figure, and she said it was well into the millions. I gasped, thinking to myself, *I only want two bicycles.* So off I went down to the promenade and waited for Bubble. It was there waiting for me, and I told it that this emerald was too expensive. Had it got anything less alluring? It bounced back to the clouds and came back with a diamond necklace, so I took it, but I told Bubble I would go to a different jeweller now as no doubt my name and profile would have been on CCTV. I went to Soho the next day and entered a prominent shop, and showed the necklace.

I was immediately shown into a room with two men with white gloves on who were looking at the diamond necklace.

"This is definitely a stolen necklace from Tiffany's; where did you get it"

I was flummoxed and didn't have an answer prepared but said I was given it to get money for it and I would get 10%.

"We are not going to phone the police," said one of the jewellers, "and will give you £250,000 in cash for it. Is that okay?"

I knew it was worth double that money, but as it stood, I accepted it and went on my way. When I got to Eastbourne station, I noticed the same people I had seen in Soho and began to get anxious. When I got outside and hailed a taxi, three men approached me and, within a split second, were fired at from the sky. I quickly got into the taxi and returned home. I knew it was a bubble; it had followed me all the way to London. The next day I went into a bike shop and bought two exactly identical bikes. Bubble was waiting outside, and when I came out of the shop with the two bikes, the salesman asked if I was going to be okay. I told him it was fine; I would get in the middle of both bikes and carry on. When I reached the promenade, Bubble appeared and tried to sit on the bike, but its legs were pointing in the wrong direction, and its hands were on the handlebars. I reached into the rucksack on my back and took out a pencil and paper, and drew how I thought it should look. It understood and pulled out its legs and reinserted them in another position. So now we were all set, and both took off along the prom without realising that everyone could now see a bicycle without a cyclist.

So, I decided there and then that I would write a children's book about my experience, but for obvious reasons keeping it within the right spectrum for children, and by doing that, I could release the guilt I had for passing on the name of Tiffany's. That night, as I closed the curtains, I noticed a bright light in the sky, and Bubble was outside at my window sill.

"We want more places to find diamonds," it said, in a muffled kind of way. This was not my friend Bubble. Where was it?

My reply was simply to look at diamond mines, but this drew a blank. There was no communication, so I got out my atlas and, leaning into the window, showed the diamond mines in South Africa, South America, and so on, but still no communication. It left me feeling puzzled, and it bounced away, but within seconds it reappeared and said, "You are the chosen one to find the diamonds in the shops," and I said, "No, I will not help you steal diamonds from shops all over the world. You must find a diamond mine."

The reply took a while, and it said, "We have exhausted all the diamond mines in the world. Now it is up to you."

I quickly closed the curtains and ran into my bedroom, unable to face the windows

I turned on the TV and watched the news. There was no more news about the diamond thieves. I then started to prepare my children's book as now I felt this was the only way to get my story across to everyone as now I felt harassed and blackmailed into letting the balloon-type creatures attack each shop to get their diamonds. As I ventured out in the morning, I could smell the presence of the bubble: I knew it was somewhere with me. I had written a few chapters of my book and, as I went to the supermarket, was thinking of ways of illustrating it. Whilst walking along the road with my shopping bag, I noticed a few people ahead of me in a crowd and found myself crossing the road as their eyes and body language presented a threat. Suddenly, as they began to approach me, sparks flew out of the sky, and they were halted in their tracks simultaneously. I rushed by them and headed for the supermarket. I could hear ambulances in the distance and curiously went outside to see the carnage. There were bodies all over the place, and I looked up to see if I could see anything, but nothing appeared. However, I could still smell the presence of the orange ball. When I had finished shopping and headed home, now littered with police asking passers-by for any information, I decided to go home, close all the curtains and finish my book. I tried to get myself a publisher to take my story on. Some said it was too dark for young children, but teenagers could handle it. So, I published it myself with drawings and called it *Bubble and Squeak Adventures*.

Some of the schools didn't want it as they also said it was on the dark side, but other places did. Dentists loved it, and so did GP practices and other waiting room specialists, for some reason. Apparently, it managed to take the reader away from their pending treatment, which I was very happy about.

One day a father in the UK travelled to the US with the book. Unknowingly his son had picked it up at his local dentist in the UK. His son put it in his backpack for travelling. The father had taken his son to the dentist with him because of childcare issues, and as Daddy was in the dentist's chair, the little boy, called Norman, had found a copy of *Bubble and Squeak* and began to read and enjoy it. When Daddy had finished his treatment, Norman decided he hadn't finished the book and decided to take it with him in his lunch box. When they had landed and got home, Norman ran upstairs to read the rest of his newfound book. Dad, who was called Mike, worked for the CIA. He was married to Melos, who was from Mexico. Melos appeared, coming through the front door, kicking off her heels and undoing the necklace around her neck.

She asked Mike about his day and whether she was going to be kept up all night with his shouting about the bubble-like creatures in the UK. This was classified information, and Mike grabbed her and said, "This is no laughing matter."

She dismissed him and shouted upstairs for Norman to get ready for dinner. Mike went back to his computer and typed in a few letters, which brought up a page relating to unidentified objects in the UK killing people and animals with their fumes: a total of two thousand animals and 200 humans over a period of five years. They still did not have any idea who or what was killing these animals and were afraid that this would get out of hand. They were already sending drones and other aircraft over these identified areas of England, but nothing had come of it.

The telephone rang, and it was Mike's boss telling him that he was appointed to go over to the UK again, but this time to look for extra-terrestrials in certain areas and come back with some answers. Now the same thing was happening in Scotland, and the British Government were wanting answers. However, this had to be kept a secret.

Mike packed his bag, and off he went to the UK, disembarking in Scotland. He was met with a variety of agents and police officers who took him to a hotel for a briefing.

Mike acknowledged that he had no idea what was killing the livestock of this farm in Sussex and the two farmers that were killed outright with intoxicating fumes, and even though they had sent forensics down there to clarify who, what, when, nothing had transpired.

Scottish agents told Mike that China had expressed an interest because, apparently, the same thing was happening there but too close to their nuclear fuel plant. Mike said that he had only heard of the UK having this problem, but then someone at the back of the group of men said, "It's been happening in the US for a long time, but we used the UK when it happened over there as a decoy."

"So, this is a nuclear accident?"

They all agreed and accepted a phone call to visit China within a couple of days.

In the meantime, I went down to the prom and saw Bubble and asked about the two different personalities, the cycling one and the windowsill one. Bubble said that there were many bubbles from the master ship, and it was shocked that one had approached me and that he would do something to stop it. The night was drawing in, and it asked whether I could get the bikes from the shed in my garden to cycle on the prom again.

"So, we have a nuclear accident on our books," Mike said openly to everyone, which gave many people a shiver down their spine, "this is now going to affect the world," he continued, and all of them began to shudder with fear of the unknown.

Meanwhile, Norman was reading his book on his bed back home whilst his mother got ready to receive a babysitter so that she could go out with friends dancing. She was very good at the salsa and was eager to get away. Norman sat downstairs on the settee, waiting for their babysitter with his book.

"What's that book?" she said. "I haven't seen that one before."

"Oh, it's a school book I like to read now and again," he replied.

She had never seen him take so much interest in a book before and tried to lean over him to find out more, but he dashed it out of her way. At that moment, the babysitter arrived, and Norman's mother was out the door looking forward to her class. The babysitter's name was Allie, and she got on with the washing up and watched Norman read his book.

"What are you reading? A school book?"

Norman said, "Well, no, actually, it's from my dad's dentist. I took it, but will return it one day, I promise. It's all about UFOs killing people with toxification."

"Oh, that doesn't sound like a dentist's book at all, especially when people are having their teeth out. No wonder you are interested in it. Does Mike know you have this?"

Norman hid the book under his pyjama top and said, "NO," as he rushed up the stairs.

A few hours later, when Norman was asleep, Alli went to check up on him and found the book on his bed. After tucking him up, she took the book and began to read it herself in a chair next to his bed which carried the light from the hallway. When she got to the part about the bubbles actually taking the last breath out of the animals, she put the book down on his bed and went downstairs.

Within moments, Mum arrived home. She asked if everything was okay, and Allie said, "Everything is okay, honey, but I am wondering whether that bubble book is good for Norman to read, you know, lots of deathly things in there." With that, she went out the door and started her car.

Norman's mother looked up the stairs and started to take off her shoes, and poured herself a glass of wine. After drinking half her glass, she went upstairs and picked up the book, which was now on the floor of Norman's bedroom, and began to read it. Halfway through, she was upset at the gruesome activity of Bubble and Squeak and put the book under the seat of the couch. She took herself off to bed and waited for Mike to ring her early the following morning.

Mike was now diverted to India as there was a report of people killed at their nuclear energy plant, and even with security cameras they could not find out why or how animals and people were getting killed by intoxication. Whilst in the air over India, Mike rang his wife as she slept. She was woken up by the ringing but also by Norman searching for his book.

"Hello darling," Mike said as she picked up the phone by her bedside. "Sorry to ring you so early, but I have been drafted to India on a new mission."

With that, Norman came into her bedroom and demanded that he have his book because Allie had taken it, and he wanted her number to ring her to get it back. Mike heard what was going on and said, "What is he talking about?"

The mother's reply was, "The book he brought home from school, which I am going to report about today because it is far too controversial for a youngster to read."

Norman said it was the best of the best book about a bubble just killing people.

Mike said, "Okay, well, I will leave that with you, my love. Catch you later. I hope you manage to sort this out."

His wife said okay and put down the phone. Turning to Norman, she said that the book was highly inappropriate for him to take to school and he should not have brought it home. Norman said, shouting at her whilst he went up the stairs, "I got it in the dentists, not school," and he got ready for school.

Mike went to a meeting in India with colleagues from the UK, USA, China and now India. At the meeting, they showed clips of bubble-like creatures managing to kill people in their way with their fumes, which were very difficult to pick up on the radar. It was only when they had killed someone that one could see their outline.

"An orange bubble," one person in the nuclear objective committee said out loud. This now was highlighted, with Presidents all over the world and Prime Ministers too. It was a top-secret event.

Then the comment of his wife started to nag Mike. Norman has a book called *Bubble and Squeak*, and it kills people? Is this possible? Did I hear my wife correctly?

As Mike went to sleep that night, he let his mind think about home and his son, especially, and remembered the book where his wife referred to "bubble-like creatures". Mike began to get sweaty, and his heart rate increased, so he rang his wife. She answered almost immediately because it was 8.30 a.m. in the US, and she was just getting in the car to drop Norman off at school.

"You okay,? she said in a loud voice as Norman sat in the front seat.

"That book about the bubbles: has Norman still got it?"

She asked Norman, "Have you got that bubble book?"

"I was going to take it to the school today but forgot."

"And I suppose you found it under the couch?"

"Yes, Mom," he replied and showed her the book in his case.

"Yes, honey, I have it. Why?" she asked her husband.

"Oh, nothing. Hey, drop Norman off at school, will you? And I want you to read that book to me".

"OK, honey."

Norman flung his hands in the air and said, "It's not a school book; I found it in the dentists."

"That's okay, honey, let me sort this one out." They both drove off to the school.

When Norman's mother got home, she reached for the book in her bag and curled up on the settee and rang Mike, who had just touched down in India. When she rang him, he was at the airport and asked a member of the airport staff to help him find a good spot to listen to his phone. He was shown into a room and spoke to his wife.

"Read this book to me, please," he said.

His wife complied without hesitation and said, " Once upon a time..."

His reaction was, "Please take this seriously," and so she relayed the whole story of the book.

When she had finished, he asked when the book was published and by whom and who the author was.

He said his thanks and that she was to tell no one, and she confirmed that his dentist had the book.

"Keep that book safe," he said.

"I will," she replied.

Within seconds of receiving that phone call, Mike had ordered his dentist to leave the building and everyone else in the 12-storey building in the US. There were film crews taking pictures; there were photographers taking pictures. No one was allowed in the building, as his wife watched television. Mike couldn't tell his colleagues exactly why he had done this, but he did give a grave report that someone had planted the book in the dentists for him or his boy to read, and that this book revealed the true nature of the findings.

Mike was summoned by the CIA to give his reasons for this bizarre behaviour at his dentists that morning and told him about the book relating to orange bubbles killing sheep with intoxication.

"This is no coincidence," he told everyone. "This was left there for me to read, but by chance, my son got hold of it, and *bang*, he was entranced."

The CIA asked what was next, and Mike said, "We travel to the UK to reveal where this all started."

"How do you know where?"

Mike said that the author was from East Sussex and visited an old lady in the country who lived on a triangle. "That shouldn't be hard to find," he said, throwing his arms in the air whilst everyone else looked disillusioned.

"OK, everyone, off to the UK. Captain, we are in your hands."

Within hours the plane was all set to land at Gatwick Airport, and during the 12-hour flight, each and everyone had a map outlining East Sussex, and every triangle in the countryside was outlined. They managed to capture 46 triangles in East Sussex. Whilst all this was going on, some were trying to find the publisher, who had since died and had folded up the industry. Hence it was difficult to find the author under the name of Sian Jenkins, a Welsh name.

Whilst all this was going on, all the searching and pontificating on how or why this book materialised in Mike's dentist, many spoke of all their dentists and asked all of them to look closely at books left in their waiting rooms, whilst countries like India and China wiped them out completely, throwing dentists out on the street, along with their patients. Dentists thought they had been targeted.

There was a great expanse of drones. Drones were to be used everywhere, and now even satellites were being organised by the tech team on board. When the plane landed at Gatwick Airport, all 46 sites were recognised in East Sussex, and helicopters were there to take passengers to all triangle-type junctions in East Sussex. Mike had asked his wife to teleprint the book to him, and for the first time, the scanned item was now on show. A tent had been put up for them to meet and discuss in forums, and the book was now on show amongst all the delegates appointed to find and kill the alien creatures.

The book's first page showed a happy bubble with another happy bubble on top, disjointed but fixed, and it showed an illuminated blue badge on the larger of the two bubbles. Turning the pages, one could see the happy couple bumbling along until they reached a fence and couldn't go through, so they had to use the lane instead, which led down to a cave which they went into. But the next day, a more sinister element appeared when they emerged from their cave to find a farmer and sheep in their way. They sprayed them with a translucent liquid that they carried inside their balloon-type form. The farmer and his flock were killed outright. The book displayed many of these activities, so the book was closed, and everyone gasped.

Meanwhile, the drones and the helicopters were out in the skies looking for a triangle and came back with nothing. Mike read the book again and said, "Look, it says that this is the only house around because she was frightened and didn't take the pathway but used the rockery instead to get to the car, which now was in a lighted position. The old lady she cared for was the only one on the triangle, don't you see?" He sounded exasperated.

Drones were everywhere now in East Sussex, everywhere they could be, and they were annoying everyone. They couldn't find this triangle. So the head of the CIA said he wanted to see any plans showing alterations in the countryside over the last ten years and waited for the plans to arrive. Mike's son Norman was asking everyone about his book and wondered whether his mum had finished with it. She replied, "That is a very special book, so I cannot give it back to you."

"Well," Norman said, "I was waiting to go into school today and heard that Miss Watson's sister worked at Dad's dentist, and they all were thrown out of their office yesterday, over some darn book – was it my book, Mom?"

"I don't know, really I don't, son; just try and forget it now."

Norman ran off into the house, and two men appeared at the front door. Without hesitation, they pushed their way in and asked her where the book was. She reached under the sofa and gave it to them. They were startled as they knew how much this book was worth, and it was just hidden under the sofa.

"Go," she said, "just go." She tried to get hold of Mike but couldn't get through, so she put the phone down and started to pack, stuffing her things into her bag. Norman found her in the bedroom and asked whether he should do the same. She nodded, not telling him about her experience a few moments earlier. They left in the car to her sister's house in Chicago, knowing that the scanned book was already on her email account.

Mike could see that she had rung him and tried earnestly to get through but couldn't. The team was camped out at a local girl guide camp which was near the 'triangle', but they had no idea. The drones were doing their stuff, picking up all sorts of abysmal fly-tipping and flooding. The town hall had been working overtime and had found land before it was built on and, indeed, may have had a clue to its whereabouts.

When all this was kicking off, I had no idea of the upsurge in the investigation. I was visiting a well-known gardening shop in the vicinity of the triangle at the time when I saw three large jets go over and around 50 drones all at once descend on the gardening shop. We were all asked to leave the premises immediately. I relied on my friend to drive, and as we did, we saw soldiers in their hundreds, it seemed, appearing around the place looking around. Some were armed. Then we saw men or women in those white suits used for chemical warfare. We wondered whether this was for a film. Then it suddenly occurred to me: what if it was an extra-terrestrial, like the one I saw that night? What if? As we were escorted out, I wound down my window and asked to speak to someone in charge. I was immediately told to follow everyone, or else. I began to shake with terror, wondering: what if there was something meaningful in my book? Perhaps it was true.

We couldn't hang around outside, but I asked to be left there as I had to see what was happening, but my friend was too shocked to carry on. I waited and waited, and the guards at the beginning of the lane were keen on stopping everyone, so I decided to take a shortcut through the woods. Dressed in blue jeans and a jumper handbag thrown diagonally across me, I set to the task of trying to reach someone because I was aware that this was real: my book or something must have prompted this to happen. It was like a jungle trying to get through all the trees. I remember there was a bridle path, but it was so overgrown. Then I heard something, and it was coming towards me. I just managed to throw myself into the trees as three horses, all saddled up, came past me. There were shrieks from children to follow; they were being chased by men in white suits. I let the children pass me by and then came face to face with someone in a white uniform and a head bag with a see-through plastic patch on the top of the mask. He told me to go back and shouted, "Go, go," and I shouted out, "My name is Sian Jenkins; I need to speak to the officer in charge," but he was relentless and told me to go back.

I had no choice but to follow his instructions and found myself in a clearing where there were young girls with their ponies. I began to give a leg-up to some of the girls to get on their ponies and walked with them out from the traffic queues. I decided to go and have a coffee in a shop nearby. As I went in, the women in the coffee shop said how awful it was that everyone had to leave the gardening centre and how people from the army were rough with them. I sat down and looked around whilst asking for a pot of tea for one. Having done that, I looked up: there were three men who came into the shop. All three were American and asked for particular coffees.

"We only do one coffee here, love," one waitress said, looking at them awkwardly.

"That will be just fine. Three takeaways, please."

I looked up at one and asked whether if I wrote a note, it could be passed to the managing officer. "Why, yeah," said one, so I wrote my note telling them what my name was and that I had information for them that may help find what they were looking for. I closed the note, as I had no envelope, just a little notepad that I used for shopping, and gave it to one of the men. They waited for their coffee, and then off they went. I saw them walk off in the distance and stood up to watch them get into a Jeep parked on the pavement. I watched one of them crumple up my note and throw it away. So, I sat back down with sadness in my heart and contin-ued to drink my tea. Then I left, as I knew a bus was due very soon and out in the country buses don't come very often.

Around the third or fourth day after this, I was cleaning my windows and looked over my shoulder to see a large black car sitting outside my flat. I thought they had just stopped at the corner Sainsbury's to buy cigarettes, and so I carried on with the windows. In the reflection, I could see two men get out of the car and walk towards me. One asked, "Are you Sian Jenkins?"

I replied nervously with a "Yes".

"Would you like to come with us?"

Of course, I didn't have to say anything and had my keys on me, so I just nodded and followed them. My neighbour was looking out of his window and started to film me getting into this rather lavish black car. Once in the car, the men asked whether I was comfortable and took me to a hotel. I had never seen this hotel before and began to get hesitant about where we were and what they wanted. When the car stopped, I was searched with a machine that looked like a tennis racquet and then led into a room sat down with five other men, no women. I was shown a glass of water together with a tissue.

"Do you know why you are here?" one of the men asked.

I said, "Yes, I do, sir."

"Would you like to tell us, in your own words?"

"Yes."

I started to tell them that seven years ago, I was looking after an elderly lady. When I left her house, I saw a balloon-type creature make its way towards me. It wanted to go through a gate, but it couldn't, and that's when I decided this had a mind of its own. So, I drove around the triangle to see if it came out the other end, and it did. I waited for it to cross the road, and it acknowledged me for doing so. I drove off.

When I had finished the story, another officer asked me, "Were you frightened?"

"No, I was inquisitive; but I became frightened when I realised it may have been an encounter with an alien."

"Did you tell anyone?"

"Yes, I told friends, but I said it was an orange light, hoping in a way that they had heard about it and wasn't the only one; but no."

Then another asked, "Have you seen this object again?"

I answered no but then added to that question. "I have Parkinson's disease. We are subject to hallucinations, and so I kept this to myself because people wouldn't believe me." I hesitated as I had seen the object before and didn't let on that it was always with me and was guilty of blowing up every conceivable place that held diamonds.

The officer whispered to another: "Eight years."

"Tell us about the book you wrote. Why did you write it?"

I told them the reason was that I wanted someone else to say that had happened to them, but no one came forward until now, and when I saw the army, I knew that it was something to do with this.

"In your book, you talk about it disappearing underground."

"Well, I made that up. I needed to have a home for it, give it a reason to be alive."

Together, the men all looked at me.

"That will be all; thank you very much for now."

I was then shown the door and ushered out of the building and into the black car waiting outside.

Unbeknownst to me, the men chatted together, and Mike, whom I had not met yet, appeared and asked about the outcome of my meeting. He still dwelled upon the fact that why was that book in his dentist's surgery. "Why did she write about it going underground, having said she made that up? It is abundantly clear that these alien types were collecting minerals used in warfare with liquid nitrogen. We have uncovered specimens here in this area, and the whole place is radiating fuel everywhere. If there was a spark, the explosion could reach us here; we need to evacuate the town."

I was dropped off in the car, and just as I was getting out, one of the men asked me if I had family in the area. I told him no. I didn't ask why, and the car drove off. When I got inside my flat, I began to ask myself why I didn't say this or that and why didn't I challenge them all. How dare they pick me up without a by-your-leave and sit me down without any information? I was so annoyed with myself. Then my neighbour Archie came to the door and started to ask questions. I opened a bottle of wine and sat down with him, trying to piece together what happened, knowing that he didn't understand a word. I began to think he thought that I might be a spy, so I let him think that.

Within the hour, there was a broadcast on the TV saying that we all had to evacuate if we lived in zones A, B and C. I was in C, so I decided to get in the car and go up north, but unfortunately, so did everyone else, and there were bottlenecks everywhere. I drove back home and sat down in my sitting room. I knew that the object was still out there hovering; I could still smell the fumes.

Out of the blue, I had a phone call, and the person on the other end said, "Hi, this is Mike; you don't know me, I am part of the organisation that questioned you today, and I apologise for not introducing myself."

I replied, "This is nice to hear from you; at last, someone personable."

Mike also asked what zone I was in and whether I was going to be evacuated, and I said I was waiting until the traffic got better.

"I will send a chopper to get you. I have an address and will send it now. If it can't land, then we'll use the winch."

I said in a very low voice, "Okay," and started to look outside.

I got my jumper from the car and my handbag and waited, and there it was, the biggest helicopter I had ever seen. Down came a man who beckoned me towards him. He just grabbed me, put a strap around me and within seconds, I was in this helicopter with around eight or nine personnel.

The helicopter was in the air for a good two hours, and finally, when it landed, I had no idea where it was at all until I saw the mountains of Snowdonia in Wales. We all got out quite quickly together and rushed towards a house or hotel as it was beginning to rain. Mike greeted me by the door and said, "Hey, Sian, I am so glad that we have met and that I have managed to find you at long last." I was overwhelmed by all this and just nodded.

I was ushered once again into a room, but this room was a bar and had an open fire. Many of the men were already tucking into beer and crisps. I sat down near the fireplace and began to unwind. I was asked whether I would like a drink. I asked for a cup of tea which Mike brought over to me; he had a beer. I then began to formulate stuff in my head to ask him, but before I could, he asked me if I knew what was going on. I said, "Well, it's obvious that something major is happening, and this happened where I met the balloon-type creatures, so yes, I would like to know more."

Mike then started to tell me that for many years they had been investigating occurrences around nuclear plants and found that nothing was showing up on their equipment until one night, when they realised that this particular balloon object was trying to open a valve in the nuclear energy component. But this wasn't just in the US; this was happening everywhere – India, China, the UK...

I interrupted him and said, "But there was no nuclear plant in East Sussex."

"Oh yes, there was, because they were building one, storing their findings, building up a cache of components in order to make a nuclear bomb. This was done underground."

"So, my book was true," I said to Mike, and he said, "But there is one question I need to ask, and that is, how did it get to my dentist's surgery?"

I said that I had no idea but was glad it did. Mike asked again whether I had any communication with such aliens, and I gave him a confident "No". The mood began to change within the room as now I was no longer a guest anymore but a prisoner being asked stupid questions, as if I was harbouring a squidgy balloon-type creature in my home. I was shown to my room and pushed in, and the door was locked.

Unbeknownst to me at this time, my flat was being ransacked, and my car was also. However, one of the searchers did come across a box of books, around three of them, and all the cuttings and information I had collected writing about my encounter: how I found the gate locked a year later, knowing that the farmer had died and his sheep too by fumes and that his wife who had Parkinson's couldn't cope and was taken to a care home nearby, and the farm left to ruin. All this information was in the box, which now sat on a desk somewhere in this building.

My books were handed out to people around the table for a reference point, and certainly, seeing the leaders from China, India, the USA and the UK referring from it or to it was quite startling. After three days in my room cell, Mike knocked on the door and asked me to get ready to go downstairs because they had found a box of information that naturally excluded me from being involved with an alien. I put my scarf on and shoes and went downstairs where all the dignitaries were sitting. I greeted them one by one and sat down.

"Sian," the Chinese chap said, "we have looked into this box of information and realise that you put together your book for it to be noticed. You wanted everyone to read it and do something radical, but that never happened. Tell us about your experience with the death of the farmer."

So, I related the case when the farmer died a few months after my experience, as did some sheep too, but the funny thing was the gate was shut and bolted and locked, with signs from the District Council telling everyone using it would be trespassing. That gate was always kept open, and I wondered about that. I said that I understood the farmer's wife was taken to a care home.

"What care home is that, please?" one of the officers asked.

I told them it was around the area and that I was sure they could visit for more information if they wanted to.

Mike stood up and stared at me, "Will you come with me to see this lady's care home? I would like to see."

I replied that it would be great to visit her because there were unanswered questions. The next day, Mike and I and a few others got into a helicopter and flew back to Sussex. Everything had cleared now, and there was no danger, so I, Mike and the army personnel were able to travel up to the home where she lived. Her name was Jean, and her husband was John. They had no children and had a few animals, goats, sheep and cows. After John's death, Jean couldn't cope anymore, so she decided to live out her days in a care home facility just up the road. Mike and I arrived at the home and went in to speak to the manager. Mike took over, with his American accent, and asked if we could see her room, which we did. We asked about her well-being. The manager told us that Jean would retire to her bedroom around 9.00 every night and watch the sunset from her room, but then she developed Alzheimer's, and it progressed very quickly indeed. We were asked whether we would like a cup of tea and Mike asked if we could drink it in Jean's bedroom as he wanted to see the countryside.

"So, the farm was taken away from them and given to the council," he said to me.

I replied, "Well, yes, the whole farm."

We both looked out the window, looking at the trees and the South Downs, and Mike pulled out his phone.

"OMG, he said can you see what I can see?" He pointed to vine trees in the distance, and there, bobbing up and down, was an orange ball, just going in and out of the vine trees. He rang someone.

"John, it's Mike: I got something. Switch your camera on," He videoed the orange ball amongst the vine trees, and it was coming our way. Halfway through our tea, we noticed that the 'bubble' turned to the right and was just out of view. We looked at the other window but couldn't find it. I looked up, and the airspace was full of drones. Mike put an earpiece in his ear and began to talk to someone who was operating a drone. Then on Mike's phone, we could see that the drone was chasing the orange ball through the vineyard. The ball was racing and bouncing; it was really caught unaware. Then suddenly, a spark of lightning attacked the drone, and it broke up in the sky.

Mike shouted, "Get the source, get the source," and rockets were fired at a light in the sky, which missed. I was cowering under the bedclothes at this point because I was afraid of getting the fumes in my lungs and being asphyxiated. Mike rushed downstairs and saw the staff looking out the windows.

"Stay away from the windows," he said, and outside he went. Another drone had picked up the orange ball, and Mike was now following the drone to the resting place of the ball. I reluctantly stood on top of the wall to see if I could see anything but saw Mike chasing the ball, the drones following him and lots of army personnel from the other direction, and then rockets aiming to capture or stop that beam of light that may have been an alien ship up above. I could no longer hear Mike's voice, and the drones were firing on the orange ball, coupled with rockets at the light in the sky.

Mike's head appeared in the vine grove. He was gasping for air, holding his throat. I shouted, "Give him oxygen, now," and a team heard me and ran to get him.

Mike was carried back to the care home wearing an oxygen mask whilst a soldier carried a tube of oxygen. Mike lay down in a room and said the fumes were obnoxious, but he managed to get away from it. He said that it turned on him and ended up chasing him until the drones came to his rescue. At that time, all the drones were sending messages as to the whereabouts of the orange ball whilst the light above was sending lightning strikes to everyone, including the drones on the ground below.

"We have made a breakthrough," Mike said to someone in the team, "Let's stay with this."

Helicopters flew over, taking pictures, but the lightning strikes from a vessel above kept happening. Mike called the helicopters to stand down, which they did. The drones were being hit accurately one by one, losing us the time to see where the orange ball lived. Then out of the blue came four aircraft. I don't know their specific names, but each of these aircraft was so quick and powerful; they were there to kill the alien ship. One after one, they fired on this light and eventually got it as it crumbled and dropped to earth. Then in a flash, they were gone: all four of them. Mike ordered that only men with nuclear protection could visit the site of the alien ship.

"Looks as though they, the aliens, moved when Jean moved." They had never left the site. All the parts of the stunned aircraft were loaded into a truck, and diggers were brought in the dig up the vineyard to see what was underneath the ground. Mike said that even though now he realised that I had nothing to do with this alien, he still wanted me around and to return to Snowdonia with him and other officials because he still didn't know how that book ended up in his dental surgery. I said that I had no idea and that there must be a logical explanation. We waited for a helicopter to get refuelled, and off we all went back to the cold mountains of Snowdonia, where all the information was being held around the world, guided by my children's book.

I was back home in Sussex now after the evacuation, safe in my surroundings, albeit I was worried about repercussions after I realised that there was an alien vessel, starship or whatever looking over the orange balloon-type creature and whether my car was noted or me giving a wave to say it was okay to pass. During the afternoon, Mike rang me and asked me to write down how many books were printed and where they were sent. I told him that I couldn't afford to have a lot printed, so I printed the minimum of 20.

"Five were in the box. You have the others I sent out to schools, which returned them due to the fact that they were deemed too violent. So, twelve were never returned from dental practices and GP surgeries. Just how one managed to get to your dental practice, I don't know. Is there anyone working in your office with a connection to the UK, I wonder? Or is there someone or something happening outside this situation that placed the book there? It had to travel by plane, didn't it? And it got here, and then your son picked it up and thought it was wicked and got so immersed he took it home, and that is where the drama started."

I began to ask Mike a series of questions about his dentist, and he said that he was there a week prior for an assessment, but without his son; his wife usually took him to school. The book didn't show itself at that point but did the second week when his son turned up.

"That particular book is with HQ at the moment, still in Snowdonia."

Mike began to tremble, and I began to think over and over if there was a marking on that book that may erupt into something that we didn't know about. Mike rang Snowdonia and spoke to someone and asked them to put a radiation detector over the bubble book. The person did, but one of them gave a signal that it was contaminated. The book was taken away and put in a metal container downstairs in a safe place before examination.

Mike began to look at the sky and wondered whether there were aliens hiding in the clouds and called in the jets to investigate. No sooner had he called them than they were there doing a sortie in the skies above, and, POW, they got one. Mike ordered that the book be brought back to the office by a man dressed in a white suit. He checked the book again, and no contamination was seen. So, Mike concluded that there were signals given to the book; but how would that allow the book to have come his way? Mike ordered a search of all people travelling to Chicago from the UK over the previous eight years, as well as those that worked within the country. The men set to work, and over a period of time, they came up with the same name over and over again. This was a dentist who worked a block away.

Mike rang the dental suite, but the man, called Albert Walker, had since left, and through data protection, the dental team weren't allowed to give any information away. Mike and two men gave the dentist surgery a visit and, in no time at all, ascertained who it was and where he was living. The three men travelled to a place outside Chicago and found a log cabin near a river. When they got there, Mike noticed that all the gates were wide open and that there were plenty of trees surrounding his cabin. As the men approached the door, Mr Walker asked through a tannoy system who it was, and Mike told him that he had an ID and wanted to talk to him about recent alien activity. Mr Walker came to the door and said, "Well, I guess you had better come in," and promptly sat down on a couch, offering his hand for his guests to follow suit. Mike asked him why he had all his gates wide open, and he said it was because they never shut properly. Then questions were asked whether he had noted any bright lights in the sky or any orange balloon shapes floating around his site, collecting dust particles from the floor, that had a strange toxic odour that could kill if inhaled. Mr Walker looked puzzled and said he didn't know what on earth they were referring to and that he retired from dentistry some five years ago, though he still did some casual work. Mike interrupted and asked if he worked for MT Orthodontics on 23rd Street.

Mr Walker said, "Yes, I did. Small practice, not much room for a big man."

Mike then asked him whether, when travelling back to the UK, he had picked up a book like this – and he showed him the book. Mr Walker looked over it, read a page or two and said, "I remember this book. I found it at the airport in the UK on a table and read it on the plane because I was late that day. It was a horrendous flight: the captain kept asking us all to turn our mobiles off, and it was affecting the turbulence, but it still happened. We landed an hour or two late, very shook up. Yeah, I must have left it on the plane, 'cos I don't remember bringing it home at all. I have no kids."

Mike reached for his phone and asked the team to look into the year 1996 and all the staff on this flight. He looked across at Mr Walker, who shrugged his shoulders, so Mike then asked for a list of all the staff who work for American Airlines so he could send them a letter asking them about this book.

"Why is this so important?" Mr Walker asked.

Mike said that he was afraid of radiative properties held in the book activated by an alien star. The other men around him gulped, and so did Mr Walker. With that, they all left and now awaited results from the airline crew.

Having sent all the letters out to the crew of American Airlines and waiting for their response, Mike received a call from Snowdonia. The caller was a Chinese delegate who said that a book at the airport had turned up there, sitting on a chair. It was recognised by a flight attendant who got the letter in the post, recognised it and handed it into security. Mike rang security and got the team to put a radiation pulsimeter over the book to get a reaction, but nothing. So he established that the one in Snowdonia was reactive when switched on by the mothership: did all the rest follow suit? He was not happy taking the book on board a plane and asked that the book be burnt immediately.

Mike rang Snowdonia and asked if that book and all the other copies could be burnt immediately to stop any further damage to our nuclear system. The black box containing the book in Snowdonia was taken outside and set alight. Within seconds, a flash of lightning sparked it, and the light shone and burned the field behind it and beyond. The starship then began to strike the house/hotel and surroundings, plus the fields where the animals were, as well as the mountain regions and walkers on the paths. Everyone within its vicinity had been affected. The jets appeared in no time and tried in vain to track and blow the ship up, but this time it downed two of the jets. The other two returned home as this was too powerful for them. Then suddenly, the starship disappeared, and whilst people were looking after the casualties, five or six orange balloons appeared, stinking of fuel, and made their way towards those helping people. The jets had refuelled and now did a counterattack on the balloons, but they were full of fuel and ignited when struck, which made it difficult for anyone to survive. It was the battle of all battles: no one had the right equipment to deal with the balloons, but the air force killed off as many as it could, and peace was regained in Snowdonia. The same happened in China near a nuclear plant; however, they had the equipment ready and waiting. In India, too, they did very well, as they had fighter jets that exploded the balloons full of fuel. In the States, this occurred near an airbase: it did not affect many people but gave a spectacular show of fire to everyone, which many people thought were fireworks.

It was never established how the book managed to find its way to Mike's dentist's office: it was a coincidence, maybe? However, several years later, back in the coffee shop in East Sussex, a member of the staff brought in her wedding photos, which included her honeymoon. In one picture, you can see a book stood up on a shelf behind them at the airport, called *Bubble and Squeak*. The diamond disasters were never explored, and to this day, the bubble still follows me around.

This is actually based on a bubble seen in Hankam, East Sussex.